The Sex Life of the Everyday Woman

by Kareena Maxwell

Dedicated to the enablers who struggle with the addicts they live with. A special love to the grieving enablers who are forced to examine their lives as the addict takes from (the family), and the support systems forcing both enabler and user to either leave, get help, or live with the disease of addictions.

Special thanks to Peter Douglas a New York City therapist whose specialty is family addictions.

By the time she was ten Dina Byrne Lopez believed that her life was going to stay exactly the way it was forever. She would always be the youngest of the Byrne children, her parents would always drive the 1962 beige convertible Chevy, Impala; her best friend Christine's bicycle would look and ride better than her 3-speed Czechoslovakian racer, and her father would remain a drinker of *Chivas' Regal* in the rocks with a gold rimmed glass.

In the three-level home that held her close, and in the mirrors and reflections in the glass of the dining room dish closet, she would forever be ten-years-old. The image of the glass on the sliding mirrors in the top floor bathroom, she prayed to be delivered from her boring face, her mousy brown hair and dull flat eyes.

When her first kisses came from Donald Summers across the couch in the playroom and his red hair played over and over in her mind and how the red hair went down the hall in school along with the sounds of slamming locker doors, his freckled hand went under her sweater until her 14-year-old nipples that were still too small for her "A" cup, felt sexy and quickened with joy. How could she be sure that he wouldn't tell the others that she gave out and feeling that it was hers even though he stumbled his school boy fingers on her. Had he ever felt this before? Then she found her soul mate where he rubbed her with determination and she was okay with it and felt like it was her own and that he had borrowed it. Then he rubbed harder and she opened wider and the thought was he thirsty? Would her brother walk in and catch them? Did Jesus still love her? What would the Snyder's who lived next door think of their babysitter now? Shame befouled her thoughts. Joy in her hushed feelings liberated her from the dull brown hair with a whisper from Donald: "I won't tell," was reassuring.

Dina rested her head on Donald's arm and his words were smooth. Stroking his face he pulled his hand out of her underwear with the secret touches locked up inside her. She didn't love Donald and didn't want to love him. There was no interest in holding him; to squeeze him into a closet for deep kisses in the darkened room at a basement party at Barbara Ashes.

It would be 3 years before another boy would touch Dina again. The Vietnam War would be telecast into living rooms from television sets with the injured and the death toll nightly. And it was another year later when Donald would sign up to go to war and return as a dead boy. He was undecided about his life, whether to go to the University, or to work in his father's automotive shop in Northern Levittown, New York, so he went to find himself. He took Dina's secret with him. It was as if his death freed her. Then Ralph Trotta and Josh Perotti were also killed on the television news and in black and white the streets of suburbia, New York: At the same time Dina measured 4 ounce hamburgers onto a barbecue grill and opened the garage door to let the delivery man set up cases of soda. The war, the nightly news show, became as distant as her first self-examinations in the mirrors in the Byrne master bedroom; as dusty as the gold autograph book from the 6th grade.

Television was the nineteen-sixty's voice of power. She believed the soldiers to be black and white mounds of losers and she could only love those who protested. She loved the anti-war, full bearded, tie dyed draft dodger; the college boy who refused to lose his ass to someone else's scheme of how to deal with ideological differences.

The war was sexy. Through music and clothes, it stimulated women into rebelliousness. They lost their hearts and their dignities when their men didn't return home from the marshes. They acted out instead of coping with deep sadness. Abandoned feelings hidden in spending money and decorating their bodies. Losing their minds with LSD, mescaline, and speed dropped down into the backs of their untouched throats. Dina found her heart free and wild while she supported the profitable side of the killing frenzy. Turn it on, turn it off. Watch the dispensable children dressed up as men die on the tube. Civilians screwing their way through their fears: Marching and protesting and screwing while their brothers, sisters and lovers kept the economy afloat in the America.

The Doors and *Jimi Hendrix* helped turn her inside out and when her fire was lit she gave no excuses. She touched the sky and jumped on her bed while she played basketball with her bras, as she threw them into the trash. Her hair was long and black, and it grew to where it stopped on its own. She swung it around her shoulders and let it glisten from *Prell Shampoo*. She bit it and chewed on it during go-go moments. Janis Joplin tortured Dina's longing to be held and to cry about it. Pieces of her heart were scattered around the Long Island home she lived in with her family. Janis screamed it out to all the estrogen saturated pussies that dressed for proms and waited desperately for the boyfriend to return and instead had sex with the sons from next door. Do it like it was the last time. Screw as if the bomb was going to hit Long Island any moment and where the hell is God anyway?

The flower growing purple hazed children threw away guns and bibles. They wandered the trails of the transcendentalists' like Whitman and Thoreau to examine unimaginable pain. Male classmates, Johnny Kitson,

Terence Jordan, and Joe Polito graduated from high school and left the clean walls of Levittown to fight for their country. Then they were gone. Then they were honored among the brass names on government designated walls as winners. Lousy students with twenty-year old hard-ons had their young racing hearts sated with guns. They must have known they were not coming back to Levittown. Terence stared at Dina one afternoon as he got into a navy blue car that was parked outside a small group of stores. It was August 1967 and his white skin flared with red cheeks. They never danced together. There was no time for her to lick his face or for him to find his hat on the floor next to her bed. He came home like Donald and often she wished it was Terence who had touched her. She let the music take her into the past where Cocaine Baby was just a beer drinker and Terence became a discussion of who was killed and the "did you hear about…" stories of the sacrificial lambs for the hamburger eating Americans.

The pink posey and purple tulip wall paper in her room reached right up to the vent of the central air conditioning. She kept it on with the windows open so it wouldn't get too cold. Her father would come home and turn everything off. "Whaddaya tryin' to cool off the whole damn block?" he would yell. Dina wouldn't say a word back to him, just continue to pose in front of the mirror and wait until he left to turn the thing back on: Dying soldiers peeked over both their shoulders and worked their 24-hour a day jobs as background for the rest of the world. Burn the draft card and drop your drawers. It didn't matter. Just keep the prices of oil and beef down to a reasonable rate. Somewhere Dina knew that the songs of woe and lost hearts from Vietnam were a new way for lovers to long for each other. In the bars where she wore her skirts tight and short she knew the songs by heart. It was the war style in the states to know them. To stare at a Jim Morrison poster then another one of Janis Joplin that would psychedelic young mounds to orgasm as the music thumped and strobe lights turned. At all cost, females waited for their junkie boyfriends who returned with nightmares, no jobs, and ridicule from snotty draft dodgers.

Dina bought into all of it. She lived out the lost woman life syndrome by running to bars dressed as tight as she could wear her skirts, as low as she could get her shirts, over to the south shore bar, The Lido. *Light My Fire* opened her thighs where no one could see. Then to Glen Cove to the Gold Coast bar where the Chambers Brothers *Time* beat tightened the elastic on her panties. A few beers later and she cried for the dead boys whose time had come today, before they had a chance to make a second mistake in their young lives.

1967

Dina sang with the house band at *Zoli's.* She had a loyalty to Mr. Zoli who let her into his bar since she was 17 with her ratty fake proof. Silk blouses during January nights – her bumpy nipples happily smiling at the regulars – the wasted fishermen, the Hofstra University students: Three wanted to marry her on different Friday nights. They had valid

I.D.'s and dorm rooms. Richard was 6'3"
and from Cleveland. Another Tony was
an exotic Puerto Rican from the Bronx,
with thick black hair, tan skin, doe
shaped eyes and a nose like a boxer.
Dina felt safe with all of them, even with
the fisherman, Will, who loved to
whisper about filet into her musical ear.
Will didn't know about hip music. His
hands were cut from fishing hooks and
fishing wire. He smelled of the ocean
and when he went to sleep at night the
last thing he thought of was the sliver of
sun that disappeared each day as he
watched the darkness of night rise from
his boat. When his body walked into the
shadows of Zoli's, it darkened the
possibility of seeing him. He would see
Dina first and watch her from his world.
Dina felt loved and wanted. Why did
Donald go to Vietnam? She faintly
thought one night as Richard scrambled
his dick into her. It was dark in his room.
One leg of her panties was wrapped
around her right ankle. When he pulled
out his hand and put in his dick she
couldn't recall. But he did use a rubber.
Middle America wasn't ready to
reproduce with an overly-charged
femme fatal from New York. *Coty's
Tabu* the perfume wore its time into her

collar. Richard felt sad when he was done. Her small halter top disappeared into his room. He shared one of his flannels and she took it home. He found her shirt weeks later when he was cleaning his room before returning home for Christmas break.

And her *Tabu* stayed on his sheets and he sniffed her shirt during his drive to give it back to her at *Zoli's*. He showed up at *Zoli's* wanting her again. The scent of her in his nose bypassed the beer that filled the invisible breath of the room. Her yellow shoes flip flopped to the house music. She opened her mouth but kept her lips closed. Richard wanted to open her legs as she sat on the bar stool. Behind him the Puerto Rican, Tony, came out of the bathroom. Dina smiled. He put his foot on the metal rung of Dina's bar stool. She was hoping that Richard wouldn't pull her halter top out of his coat pocket. In nakedness camouflage begins, she thought.

Chapter 2

Will sits on the curb of the road. Traffic runs past him. Dina strokes the top of his head. His crown is black and gray and curls into loose rhythmic hair, beautiful hair that she rubs and feels.

The cars dump fumes into their loving lungs. He scurries through papers. He is excited to go to the hotel with her. He can hardly find the address. He wants a taxi. He wants a beer. He wants Dina in the room alone with the sunlight wandering through the hotel window. He stops still, frozen with her hands on his head. He softens from her touch. There are things on Will's mind about the visit about Dina, his lover. He needs to see to her during the day. In a moment he is distracted. His brothers wait downtown in the canyons of New York City to see him and over the cobblestones and into the dead fish smell of Chinatown. Will is older than Dina. She watches his maturity, his grown-up-ness. He is strong. His body is solid and tan and forceful. It longs for her; to love her. He

14

is thinking of placing his finger on her mouth. He bites his lip.

Her mother died as the wind pushed through the crack of the window. Will whispered her name, Dina, the one that her mother gave her for a lifetime then his tongue along with the name went into her ear. Dry word, Wet love. At once and through her rose her mother's memory. The days and nights of making dresses that never fit right, for all the holidays that the newspapers said should be celebrated; of priming canvases that sat against the wall waiting for Monet or Lautrec to appear. His teeth now replaced his hands. Not able; unable to remember suckling. She was now letting him do that and she needed to nurture him in that way; to honor her mother again with her own breast. In the whistling came her name repeated

"Do you hear her?" she said. "Listen, she's here…my mother she's here."

He maintained his grasp on her breast, turning it to a cherry color, nipple ready to fall to the floor.

"I love you," he said.

The mother of mothers was transformed in size and defined to now a different life—the other life—primed life like her art. The two of them could make love in life in earth's window one time. Missions, different, different. The spirit renewed the lovers. Space vacuumed by deep fingers, too many to count losing track and then so alive she too was dead like her mother.

Her hair knotted from his pulls on her reining her in, winding her around his great wound. As the liquid ran out of her precious place he continued to rise so he placed his finger on the crack in the window to see if the whistling sound would stop and it did.

The departure left their lives with form. Will needs to live inside her to visit her atoms, to vie in the molecular side. He would return to Dina and she would wait for his life to return to her, but now in the place where the earth quakes and crumbles he was really in the desert and he called it home. Illicit dreams were to become the norm for her lover. He would finish her drinks; eat from her finger food from her place, placing his prints on her leaving imprints in his mind. He couldn't stop thinking about her. She wouldn't stop seeing him. His bold back, as bold as his form she touched his hydrogenated skin with her eyelashes. Dina's shoulders fell onto Will. The bed was large and he placed his mouth on her stomach under her shirt without using his hands. She smelled like honeysuckle and he knew it was perfume and he appreciated how she planned her body for him. He was her big, beautiful doll. Over her Irish skin he pronounced his love for her. He cleaned her with his mouth until his dry lips found her where she was a girl again in front of her parent's mirror. In her white skin she rolled over until he went on top until her spirit and his spirit remembered why they were together after twenty years.

Will examined her grateful for his eyes to see, happy to smell her again. The room darkened. It would have been dinner time for her son Carlito if she were home. His lips brushed hers.

"You okay?" he whispered. Will could drink the walls, closing his eyes as he kissed her. His delicious spit; the taste of his member that she missed when he was gone; all of him to be licked in time.

"Freeze your mind and put your business on the floor," she said. Will was eating a donut. The air to drink; the leaves wet with kisses of water, the dew rising out of his lonely-for-Dina place and the donut piece balanced in the corner of his mouth before he spun it back into his throat with his tongue. The food went back and forth in their mouths, fortifying. Her hair was dark, silky streams of dark water long. Long. Trapped dark hair. Youthful. Loving hair. Pulled by Will in love making, tightened by his love for her. He grabbed it. Ate it. Her legs opened like her mouth; little bird with a red beak. Then again they were in the love grasp in nature's phenomena, the human place where time stops having meaning. Will and Dina missing each other before they were done. In her groans and in her words she tells him that she has never stopped loving him. "We wanted to be lovers right away as soon as we looked we both wanted it. But we had to wait. We had to starve ourselves to death by marrying others first."

The blanket on the bed danced with little gold and blue triangles: Sixties modern safe in form, colors that didn't show the dirt. Fabric with no shadow; unrevealed and without a path for the top or the bottom of the spread. Dina rubbed her nude body from the chill then he whispered, "I'm leaving her."

"Cover me," she said. Will pulled the blanket around her. He got close to her ear; to her face. "Is it for us? Can we live together? Is that what you are saying?" Dina liked it the way it was; part-time loving with many days for planning and dreaming about the unfolding. Carlito would not like it. Her brother would not say a word, and Tony the once beautiful Tony who was now her husband had become the *Cocaine Baby* would call her a whore. The names he called her for years; the whore of the fashionable building: The fucked up bitch on the 8th floor with the mixed kid who liked the Latin dick.

A week before Will returned to his wife he wandered with Dina around sculptures in a garden of light. Navigating around the work loaded with rocks and dreams. He placed his hand inside her shirt. Inside she sang. Inside there was no world only feelings. Among the sculptures of the dreams the bond took place with them and then she said, "Do you think she would like me?"

He put his hands on her face. It was now in her that she knew and believed that she loved only him. She was in the dead love place of sleeping only with sloughed cells. And during the last night in sleep she came upon her mother. Her words were kind and long full. The vision of her mother sitting in her bathrobe dominated her waking hours; sitting in a chair, feet on the floor in front of her, smiling. There were babies crawling on the floor and then put into cribs; babies that didn't cry or soil, clean, perfect babies lying on the rug in front of the mother. Her shoulders, bare, hair looping on them. "She wouldn't want to like you," he said.

The California coast was his home with another. The faint face of Dina now in the distance was the only he could hold his life together with the wife. Will could keep his hands in two jars at one time. Dina's wet soul charged his nights when he was met with a stone wall, lime, brick – unflavored milk. He missed the soft breast, the sweet, tiny nipples; the journey of Dina's voice where they traveled to the place where they could live alone.

After four weeks of being away from the wife she looked shorter than he remembered her to be. She had done something to her hair and it clashed with her face and skin and now her smile was done in a weak attempt to reassure him of her love. She was a musical instrument he had never heard of. He was unable to tune her in. Then she stood before him happy with her changes. Changes that made her glow because of how they made her feel. Then her kiss was upon him after he had been on the plane and not eaten anything substantial. Will patted her shoulder and then wished for Dina's mouth as he looked at his wife with inquisitive squinting eyes in the sun; her cold hand on his belly working around his back up toward his collar. Three thousand miles and one-half day later and his life is unlivable.

Will married his South American Peruvian wife whom he thought he could be somewhat happy with while he dreamt of someone like Dina. He believed that he couldn't be truly happy again and that the passion and a deeper connection with a woman was gone in his life. After eating dirt the Peruvian woman looked good: Pleasant; a voice, someone to share and to listen to breathe during the night. How much sex can an old man have? How important was sex really? Sex and deep love were dead he thought. He could sit the rest of his life out in the ground with a nice woman, a lost femme and pretend to be happy. He thought.

Dina loathes the wife. She doesn't want to but she does. The wife is weak and when he says this he weakens too. Dina is ashamed for him. She loves Will. His thoughts, his skin, his armor. Feelings of embarrassment flavor her attraction with lemon maybe, or just bitter. She doesn't want it to be so. She puts her head under water and swims and swims and in between the water and the sun under the sparkling particles that light the tiny ripples in the lake.

A rainbow manifested over the afternoon city. There were words from Dina's family that it was her mother's heart and that she was asleep in her bed when it happened. The call came after with wind. The element that was truthful no matter what. Dina knew that her mother had died before everyone else did. Then she was okay with hearing her mother call her name and the wind directing her forces toward her and Will.

Out the window, past the window where the mother in spirit spoke, fences of concrete led the way back to the west where Will had rewarded himself with business improprieties and the impact these improprieties had on the countries challenged with poverty. Tones that fat Americans are secretly jealous of. Where can the truly poor go except to God; to spirit. His hands were still worn from fishing hooks: Thick and wandering fingers that made her groan. Dina could feel his hands on her in waves of

involuntary impulses during the hours of
the day since he left.

Chapter 3

On East 109th Street Cocaine
Baby placed his feet over the side of the
bed. The borrowed bed where Mrs.
Ortega's, Felix would be sleeping if he
didn't end up in the hospital with
congestive heart failure. Cocaine Baby
understood the rosaries that draped
across the head board of Felix's bed. He
was grateful for the rice and beans she
kept for him in a covered dish each night
in the refrigerator. Mrs. Ortega never
questioned him. He could stay there
until Felix came home. Cocaine kissed
the Jesus on the white plastic rosary. He
wanted a miracle. He wanted his Dina
back in his life.

He sat on the edge of the bed.
The heel of his sock twisted toward the
front of his foot. It was 11:15 AM. He
was two hours late for work. He listened
to the dog breathe deeply like an
asthmatic: A deep, soulful dog. It was
his fifth week without his wife. He
missed her and told her so. But he didn't
want to have her. He wanted to go to
the kitchen in his old home and get
Carlito's gray-speckled bowl, fill it up

with Rice Krispy Treats cereal until the snapping noises stopped: The cold milk so delicious in his swallow. He wanted to hear his son slurp milk, mash cereal in between his teeth and to take the bowl back from Carlito when he held it out toward him to fill it up with more. Cocaine wanted to obey his boy. To kiss him on his young candy head and sweep back his hair from his forehead and examine his hairline. Carlito had Cocaine's color skin and his temper. He had his mother's eyes and her laugh.

Cocaine called Dina from the projects where destroyed Puerto Rican men go to live after their wives throw them out; where they grow into half their sizes, at twice their ages, while they slump into the cemented earth. The El Barrio male resolves to dissolve before his time. "What does rehab have to do with the way I love you. I miss you. I miss our home. I miss Carlito," he said.

Dina waited for the words to stop; for the faucet to turn off. There it was again, her nightmare, dropped in between her reality like meditative insights. She could see the options, she knew the forecast. Even during the separation he could not stay away from the powder. He was high, zooted up before he drifted off the project window balcony into a powerful, edgy sleep. She could hear him slurping his face, sucking, sucking up his lips and saliva. Lemon sucks. Uncontrollable pauses, in between three-quarter thoughts. His eyes like a dying insects- wide and dark staring straight ahead as the pupils took over the face. He would lie on his back with his hands clasped across his chest. His pounding heart vibrated in her pillow; she remembered the tapping that visited the lump in her throat and then her mind jumped with his beats.

Cocaine pushed back his tears. His heart was walking in mud. His eyes were exhausted from years of a vision less life. He grabbed his stomach from the inside and it was knotted into little trysts that he couldn't understand.

Dina looked at the mounds of clothes to be sorted, to be put away. Touching waistbands and folding materials of karma, she accepted the fate of Cocaine possibly meeting his maker soon. She too often reminded him not to forget the skim milk-not 99%

but skim. He never got it, or her birthday or mother's day or Christmas. On each holiday she stopped existing. She was projected as an empty honor, like the moon when it transitions back or forward and it is empty of emotion, she became a void moon on days of meaning.

The radio was in the same mood as the day he left and the house was serene and cool and all three of their hearts were there even though they felt broken and loveless from the dizzying effects of separation. Dina would not let Cocaine rewrite the script. Not this time.

He wanted to come back to the apartment. His home for years like his mother's where he was forgiven every day for being a cocaine baby. His cut hairs swept across the oak floor, the peel and stick tiles and the tiny tiles on the bathroom floor around the toilet where accidental drops of pee turn orange. His home where his lungs recovered from the back room smell of drugs, where his mucus membranes remembered the smell of bacon and coffee on Sundays and the scent of Dina every day. He thought about her constantly. He looked away when another woman looked like her; he stared too long when another woman looked like her.

His whitening beard and seasoned elegance that attracted women to him meant nothing. His style was to not give a shit. A persona from his Scorpio rising, not stronger than Dina's Scorpio sun and Venus and the conjunctions surging into her that he lived by and that he pleaded for forgiveness, but she was now done with it all. Cocaine liked to sit on the couch and now it was five in the afternoon and he sucked on his own face, his eyes floating in his face. Desire, demanding desire was the most dependable thing about him was his desire.

Cocaine came to the apartment with a runny nose and swollen eyes. He caught Dina's window gaze: Hidden and proud, her heads were shrouded in glorious time and secrecy. He felt that her tubular, insular way was changed. He noted the back of her head that the sway had more than the usual movement to it and the way she looked down her nose with her eyes downcast was now more direct. To Cocaine there was no one like her and he couldn't think for a second that she would really leave him. He always told her that he was a nice guy and she agreed. A nice guy; decent in human ways. Kind. Good to kids, generous to her. But he had evolved into a cocaine baby who still wanted sex with her always wanted sex with her. That day with the openings in Dina's mind and body as it expanded and his wanting to touch her and nest inside her even though he was drooling and sucking his lips from terminal cocaine nervousness, from one moon to the next he remained the same cocaine baby.

"You're always gone," Cocaine said. Dina unaware of her goneness ran her fingers through her hair. He wanted to hate her for that. Her fine hair and deep emotions kept him wondering and excited about her.

"It's the poetry and you know that. It's what I do. You blow notes and I write. We're different that way," she said throwing her hair around her back like a big cat. Not one that wanted to get laid but that wanted a new tribe. "You look like shit…you're not going to my mother's funeral looking like that."

Cocaine fell back onto the couch. His favorite place to sit where he could curve his spine into the familiar cushions and where his feet touched the floor just right for the length of his legs His eyes floated, his mouth sucked a lemon. Dina hated him. Then felt sorry for him. Her back hurt from holding him up. She peeled him away a strip at a time from the bed and from the family. Cocaine returned to el Barrio that night to sleep on Felix's bed.

Cocaine and Dina are embarrassed that their lovelessness shows. Do their friends see it on their faces? Can they pretend to be happy in front of them? They want their privacy. He lets them kiss her hello and he doesn't show that he is in love, but is indifferent. She likes his indifference. She is happy that he is starting to leave her alone. Dina right now in her heart is loving Will. Her Will. Warming her sultry heart with thoughts of Will. Then the couple pretend to be married. Pretend to be in love. Others are watching. Pretending is easier than explaining;

than admitting. Cocaine is lost in many moments without Dina. He calls her on the phone. He tells her that they are going to make it. Dina pushes his hands away when he reaches toward her. He watches her breasts and wants them. He needs to smother himself into her, down into her, down into her hair and behind her neck. Dina turns away; pulls away and says, "No." He grabs her anyway. They are a virus. They are a dead Mr. and Mrs. since he took cocaine as his mistress. Then the infantile personality became the most provocative part of him. He stopped washing his clothes. Let his beauty fade away. He couldn't see from cocaine blindness that Dina was losing her lust for him. Making love was like washing dishes in cold water.

Dina, sexual, loving Dina who is grieving Cocaine's penis that now is underground. Gone forever with the adoration she once held for it. The penis she glorified and held highly in its omniscience that it moved her into deep joy. His penis that she held and played with and depended on that it was always going to be there. The days were long and sad but the penis was always there.

At the end of a day, in the middle of a Saturday afternoon when Carlito was distracted as the rice was getting micro waved, they could both depend on Cocaine's penis. She couldn't remember when she last looked at it. In a soft state; non-erect urinating looking penis. The boy penis, with beige-pink shrunken with bloated details, lines around it cylinder organ grinding penis. Her once joyful experience was now a question mark. They slept together for years and both used it so why was she now worried about the health and well being of his penis? The unattended penis; the disappearing penis. But it left her years ago when Carlito was two and three and four and five and six years old. When Cocaine came home high from the Dominican band with money and the made-to-order suits from money that was burning through the wash. The laundry was never so dirty.

The rain matched the inner juice. She looked at the bed forgetting that Cocaine was no longer allowed there. Not allowed in her bed to sleep, to love her. The blanket rose with his movement. It tangled with his legs. The pillow crumpled with his years. The

smell he left behind had started to fade:
The sweat of a man, of cocaine, of
toxins, of sex, mixing and alternating in
pleasure and disgust. When do the
wedding pictures go? When do the
junkie musician photos get taken off the
walls? Dexter Gordon clouded in smoke,
the black and white photo that she
hated. Cocaine's heroes were not hers.

Chapter 4

The East River runs Dina's life with its beauty. It flows wildly with its borders reinventing itself with the spring season. It minds her business. She cries to see the other side that looks so beautiful from the drive. The river takes her power. Two-faced Manhattan allows the Hudson and the East Rivers to compete. Dina sighs like the bodies of water, relieved as one leaves and the other rushes toward her. The changing season chastises minute glaciers thrashing them into the ocean clearing its view while refusing blockage or disloyalty. The treeless people walk by the dead river. Unloved, yet adored. Climbing its way into the Atlantic, sicker than the deep waters of Coney Island but revered and sought after.

Before she was born she knew she was alive. She remembered before the beginning the death of life. Love would be her realm of consciousness: Finding understanding, knowing, experiencing, and protecting love from the angles of hate and abandonment. Her mission was to conquer it and to love anyway. Anyone. Open her heart and close her legs. Then open her legs and close her heart, and then to open it all including the spirit.

The miles of the Manhattan as an island flattened bulldozed into flat lands. Grids created for easy living, for business ... the center of the island in boxes of neighborhoods ... the streets, and avenues, in neatly procured boxes. The hilly and rocky island from overwhelmed Indians became European land not for love of man but for love of money. Grid it. Square it. Round it. Ground it. The white man found it.

Dina woke up hung over from the love mood; the dreams in the day of her lover her hero loving her on his horse. Letting her love him under his jurisdiction was true. Dina full; Dina with surprise: Her love that spidered into his sober life and spun him around. He rehearsed his plans. He pulled her into his dreams. He gave her his Vietnam pictures during his visit. They found each other after two decades of not knowing where the other was. They lost touch; lost time. When a war in South

America took him across the borders
and fences Carlito was growing inside
Dina's body. Will never forgot even after
she married Tony. And Will wrote her
letters over the years and she was
terrified of seeing him again of loving the
idea of seeing him. Dina. Sexual loving
Dina whom Will wrote to one last time. A
post card: His post card. A photograph
of his and he believed he could maybe
know her again one day even though he
was just married months ago. He never
forgot Dina. He kept her on his mailing
list the one where old friends stay on
and on. He remembered the way she
laughed and what she laughed at. When
they were loving they would laugh all
night long. Never wanting him to go, she
loved his face, his nose, and the laugh
that came out of him without warning.
His hair. Full Black. Straight. Mexican.
She loved him for looking into her eyes
while he mounted her as he put the
diaphragm in. Not once did they stop
looking into each other until dawn and
she was so excited that she could not
sleep. She could not close her eyes.
She loved him with the light of day. She
loved him into the days of working, while
washing clothes, while reading, while
going out with others, while knowing

Tony, who grew into a Cocaine Baby, and while listening to Cocaine's plans, goals, the whole damn time she was in love with Will.

It is dark when she first wakes up. The blackness is in her head; in her mind, her mind accrues with the dissolution from the day before. And she has pain with feelings unavailable to her. She is hung over from the memory: Drunk with flight of spirit with Will. The mind has been vacuumed from memory and thoughts. They fizzle daring her to look at the life she has before her. She buries her breath in her face as she turns into her pillow. Then it is soft against her full cheeks. Not her life. Not her men, but Carlito's skin barometers her living. His eyes look blind when his head is turned. But his mother knows, and sees, that her son has knowledge about her lover. Mother mumbles. Carlito hears, yet he wants more than anything to be among the deaf.

Dina loves her Carlito. Her own seed; her milky seed … her yolk. He is now life. Only one life exists for days and weeks and months. It is the one life of Carlito and Dina. There is no he. No she. Only one breath. One exhale. Their blood intermingles in thoughts of cocaine war. They battle and alienate the energy. The cereal bowl will stay empty. Carlito has become his father's guide. Carlito is his father's model. The whore, and the kid little Carl fuse into a barrel.

Carlito stands in the doorway. He looks like a man but smiles to his mother like a baby. His teeth charm his mouth. He has the look in his eyes of a young lover. Dina hopes that he is still a virgin because he is too emotional to be in love. And he with his beautiful Latin face—wide bright eyes, clear smooth skin that he shaves everyday with his father's shaving cream and his used razors that benefit by aging on the sides of the sink. The tools from the father whom he hated with the emotion of a hurt boy who is almost man enough to scream it. Then. from one day forward. When. The pain was too big and too sharp and too real, Carlito expressed himself to Dina and Cocaine and from that day on he would say what he felt. And so on the first day he said to his father; the father who rocked him to sleep when he was a baby to jazz songs, the father who ran back to the house to get Carlito's inhaler for his asthma, the father who took him to Little League for years until Carlito grew tired of it, the father who washed his clothes, the father who cleaned off his saxophone after Carlito threw up all over it. The father who showed him how to pee into the toilet which caused the little Carlito to laugh all night until he fell asleep and so he said in his now manly and resounding voice, "I hate you. Who are you to tell me when to come home when you've done all kinds of things that I will never do. Now she," he said pointing to his mother, "can tell me."

And Dina, in that expression from her baby with the charmed smile heard both their hearts die. And she could see the words melting down Cocaine's face. The tiny muscles underneath his mouth, his old smile fell downward. Words were gone. And his face fell with frost and he would have drowned himself easily into the river if he were standing next to it. He could only find the couch and then sit for the rest of the afternoon.

From the time she was a girl, Dina could remember and realized and knew with the parts of her that live inside, that never show themselves to the rest of the world that she was supposed to love Will. His life echoed inside her resonating with unfulfillment every time she met someone new. And it was the truth that each one that she laid down with was not the one. And she hoped and wanted it to be so and would search in their eyes and in the way they lived their lives that he was the one. There was constant sense that she belonged to another idea, another soul, and it just hadn't formed yet. But she knew this by a sound inside of her; a sound that was looking for its origin. She was always looking over her shoulder thinking it was he. Searching the eyes of all the others and evaluating their look at her. How would she know? And when she met him and she reconnected with him she knew because she had stopped looking at other men and there was a song inside her that flew out and never stopped. And she sang and she just knew.

In the shower as she waits and knows the truth his eyes look at her in the water and the tiles are his lips for her to kiss. His eyes now pass through the buildings and cars and airplanes and mountains: And his member, sweet and delicious rubbing against her sorting through twenty years of loss. Now the time that they have been away from each other has meant nothing. It has been sweetened and each second of touching inspires the next look, the next kiss; the next lick. Her lips caught droplets in the shower and the distance unable to destroy the pull. Tears push out of her even as she doesn't want them to. The grieving and the joy rob her of knowing where she is.

She lets Cocaine in. His need to touch her is her need to be touched by Will. All over he is on her with his cocaine breath and his cocaine spit. The touchis not Will's but she must see him in her mind to endure to fill the feelings as she tries to avoid the pain, as she tries to give an identity to the tears. But it all escapes her. She is drunk now with cocaine. He grabs her ass the way Cocaine does it. "See Will," she thinks as she rolls the words over in her mind that she frames to his house and she waits to hear back from him. She keeps her legs open and her skin planted in filaments of fibers.

"I am your Don Corleone," Cocaine says. He wants to pick tomatoes from his backyard and squeeze pods in between his fingers to check for firmness in their garden. The fruits in the vines scan him into a mature gentleman. "I am the partner you want," he says slurping his bitter, lemon lips. "I am who you are looking for I am tender." His cocaine breathis unbearable. But the available hands and his desire are ready to look for crickets before dust and now they both know that it is too late for plans.

What Dina wanted from Cocaine was to be held tightly, to be held for no reason. To be valued as a woman and feel it in his words and to see it in his touches and know it when he looked at her. She wanted to be swaddled into his heart and kept from those falling dreams, clasped, closed held closely to his hisness. He feels her breasts with no feeling. Just for him to be excited. He is the soldier raising his gun, his arms, and shooting always with the same aim. Her arms hang over the cold metal bed railing. The neighbors hear when the floor boards upstairs stop creaking. Someone, someone is listening.

"I don't want you Cocaine. I don't whisper your name when you are not here. I whisper his. I say, 'come to me and love me. Come back to us so we can love each other again.' I say, 'I miss you do you miss me?' But no, I don't say, 'Cocaine where are you that I miss you because I don't. I don't love you."

It, the anger, the love, the fire, raged inside him. He couldn't see it. Only feel his eyes glazed which were new to her. She now missed the old way Cocaine would be. Stoned, but gentle; a quiet drunk. Her lottery tickets went on the floor from the breeze he created when he ran after her. With one hand he held her neck. The collar of her shirt was ripped and dragged out of shape. With his right hand he punched her face. She was never hit in her life. Not by her mother, nor her father. Cocaine was so forceful that her lip split in threes from the smack into her teeth. She was afraid that he would rape her again. The heaviness of his thin, male body, his determined mouth as his knees forced her legs flat. Why did this excite her? Terrify her? How could he want her this way? What if Carlito walked in and saw her bleeding? A vision of him seeing his

44

father beating his mother made her tight inside. The heaviness of his determined mouth as his knees forced her legs flat made her mouth dry. The challenge made Cocaine feel like a real man. Hide. Cover. He pulled his hands off her face and she bit his hand. Blood flew across the room onto the wall dotting the floor in dark red spots. She jumped and ran out the door to the stairs that led up to the roof.

The roof was hot. She in dark midnight hair and his shining silver streaks were like the aluminum chairs. Seats to sit on and gaze into and to talk to and cloudy creeping stars on a Manhattan night were tripped over by Cocaine. He fell backward. Cocaine Baby looked at Dina the source of his light. Her eyes … he looked at … he looked into and he saw what she had been looking at for years. Now he could see the cocaine in her eyes. All along from her light into her dark and now it was theirs. Then the front right part of the chair went with Cocaine holding onto it. Over the ledge and he reached for Dina into the sky and she was reaching out long before he fell, clawing her way into the hot summer night. Her skin so wet she could slide through the humidity. The chair, she went for the chair. She growled like an animal. He was not Cocaine Baby but now he was the beautiful Puerto Rican student she had met years ago at Zoli's Bar. Innocence on his face as the unchartered experience of death was to be read from him. Over the roof, off the roof, her cocaine addiction went down and all she ever wanted was to hear him say that he loved her. She wanted to hear it from his mouth, his mind, his bowels, to say it, then to live it and to approve of her and not counter her life, and ideas: to stop belittling her movements and generosity. She wanted him to accept her to validate her and to agree and to give her time to learn and to not be criticized. To hold her in the morning in the bed as the light changed crystal lamps into prisms of color. To be nice to be loving to be adoring when they were alone and not just in front of others. And as he went off the roof with a dripping nose and a desire to take her with him, in her rage she called him and cried out, "You bastard."

And he hated her back as he tripped off the roof and the smell of

Chinese food from the corner restaurant was in him and he loved her and he realized now as his head fell backward over the plastic back of the chair that she could now be with Will and so he yelled that she was a bitch and a whore until his beautiful ethnic Puerto Rican wide bridged nose smashed inside his skull from the fall. Then, everything stopped for Cocaine Baby and it was dark and there was nothing. No Chinese food smell, no Dina to look at, no Will to hate, no Carlito to love, no couch to slump into, no cocaine to snort. Every exhale brought the release. The letting go. Exhaling was always a practice to die.

Chapter 5

Vessels dominate the city's veins. Boats, ships and yachts bulge into the Hudson River. The universe is on water. Crowns looking to see white sails: Heads like tall nipples on land falling into the cold water want to own the vista. To take it home. New Yorkers are starving to death from nature deprivation.

The mayor and the police commissioner smile. They review the day's events to the pubic media. The money media, not the truth and today New York City is one press release. It is clean. It is safe. It is fun. It is love. It is the 4th of July.

Across an overpass Dina stops. Below the cars are moving on FDR Drive. She stumbles into Cocaine in a fantasy. She remembers his floppiness, bent limbs and his curved back as he sat in the chair: The vision overlays the moving cars. His teeth are sore; his gums are pained. She is unfinished.

She walked south to the United Nations Park where it was windy. The dragon heads from the St. George sculpture were splayed on the grass. She knew by the scent of the fresh cut grass; in the sun and on the pink apple tree petals on the ground that Will was there. Talking to her in the banging of the flag poles that he missed her now in the sun while the void of his other stopped dancing. He didn't want to lose faith in his mountains; the hills of nature's sculptures, the remains of the winds and waters; the chips from the sun's crust. Dina was in love with the great St. George on his horse whose two front legs were raised as he balanced his weight on his thighs: The spear through the dragon's heart, his mouth agape at his disbelief, as he witnessed his own death. She fell deeply in love with the statue anyway; the bold silhouette that it became against the Astoria sky at dusk. Every time she looked she fell in love again and again with the heart getting pierced by the spear. Death was never so gallant; so reborn, so lusty.

Dina's daily living was pained by being in love with Will. Will who was driving his love into buckets of independent projects looking for his dream during the day to meet him when the day was finished.

In slow motion movement, like a ticking second hand on a wall clock. Words with glue on them feeling like walking in quick sand. The anti-love came in the form of a stroke. The wife. Will's wife. The call:

"She had a stroke," he began, and whatever else he said faded into *cocainville.* It equaled the unavailable Will adding to the lost woman syndrome from the war of thirty years ago. Will could have a lot of women even though he was out-of-shape, almost too old, and not the prettiest face. His belly folds over his belt, he can't cross his knees and he has deep wrinkles on his soft face. Men are a commodity. He loved his Dina and still longed for her to touch him into the darkness; into lightness. The nights are now to be met with a lonely wolf cry of aloneness as he gave to his partner, the Peruvian, with the unhappy soul. Now the wife could live out what she had been creating for a lifetime. No longer having to struggle against what she had wished for. It was here. She wanted to die. She hated life. She didn't want to dance. She hated parties. She hated birthday celebrations and anniversaries put her to sleep. The contradiction was exhausting for Dina to hear. The conflict for him was to keep his wife alive, to provide the best treatment the western world could and to try to find some meaning for it all. Now he could really forget about sex. Women who had never borne children she thought were different than women who had. The wife's happiness was wrapped up in something external where life didn't exist. Childless women couldn't get sexed right and couldn't give it back either. To connect with the uterus, the core of the woman's soul one had to give birth. After having Carlito, Dina could screw like a dog. Her cave was deep and the spirit became whole after Carlito came out of her.

Dina hated loving Will and hated him for loving this childless woman: The void soul, hated that he was so far away and hated that she needed him. She hated that the wife was in his life to distract her Will to take his time away from their time together. It wasn't the love that Dina had for Will that drove her into the depths of darkness, it was the longing, the missing, the endless dreaming the overwhelming wandering of fantasy, the remembrance and the reliving.

Dina found her love consciousness tagging along on the tap, tap, tapping noise of her lover's wife's cane, as it hit the ground, the noise, the grounding of the ugly reality of feeling and feeling that he didn't love her; just the wife; the wife with the left side of a body stiff, and spit coming down the corner of her otherwise non-sensual mouth; the right side showing and reminding Will of her potential to be a woman. Full and sexual but it was never to be. Before the stroke she was already dead. An a-sexual woman with no girlie piece that could turn him on like a man; the man that he is. He could fuck like a bull and make the sacrifice of behaving and loving a woman in a different way when he married her. So any possibility for her ever gaining knowledge on how to love, or learning how to love him, was now gone. Will was angry for the loss and guilty for wanting to be loved and for loving Dina.

Dina didn't have to be with Will to feel rejected all she had to do was to think about her father. Where are Will's fingers now? How could she call up a good memory of being with him when the memories were less than what she already had with Cocaine? She strokes her middle and sees the hair going off the roof. Her hand reaches out for him for a piece of clothing, the chair, his skin just to keep his life going a bit longer. Why couldn't he stop using drugs? Why couldn't she be woman enough for him to change for her? Tony, the dead, was alive in her. Then her face was not like it was before. In front of the mirror she could see Tony, her Cocaine Baby looking back at her. A shrunken face of a lost woman was there. Dina was more beautiful now than when she was younger: A deeper woman. She wanted to return her hands to the cocaine days. A now deleted time that would live on in Carlito and into his children. Lime green. Stand in the pool. Summon your leader who took you to bed on a whim. So her Will was now the main feed to two women who needed him. Dina, now feeling less than beautiful as the sick, cane clicking wife was more important than she was; she who just needed to be loved:

I have a heart prosthesis where my heart hung before. I have a fake heart where my real heart used to be. A cold regulated beat. A clean cut fabricated pulse.

-Dina Byrne Lopez

Dina is sending Carlito away to school. To Northern Massachusetts to know farms and cows and Denny's Restaurants where old ladies wipe down tables with buckets of ammoniated water, and stare into orange sunsets while they remember high school dances.

Carlito dreamt of finding his father's ghost in the dorm halls at night. He wanted to see Cocaine even if he had cocaine in him. If he was dizzy from his nervous system getting adjusted and his heart so fast with rhythm that his breathing was shortened, it didn't matter. Just to see him once more. To freeze along with him, marbleize his soul even to die with him. Carlito spent hours at a cemetery where the names were hard for him to say; fathers, and mothers, and some children from one hundred years ago. He imagined the pain of losing a child and realized that there could be nothing worse. The dead are lost, he thought. They are with no one. No one knows them. He decided that when he died that he would transform into an eagle—a bold wide-winged bird--and that he would soar over the peninsulas the plains and the hills and never die. And he would hide on rocks and cliffs and that he would be the father. A caring father: Carlito's father had no grave. His ashes were shaken from a bottle across the South Bronx into puddles by drains so he could float happily forever into the time of water. To mix with salt and mercury and the diamonds who live in that land.

He hated his mother for sending him away. "I'm going to run away to another city," he told her.

"I'll find you and when I do I'll give you away to the state where you can live with all the other deviants who can't understand how much their families love them." Carlito made a fist and pulled his lips across his teeth. "Want to talk about the accident?" she said.

Carlito started to cry. Then he looked away blinking away his emotions. Carlito wanted life to be one glossy pair of shoes. Perfectly heeled, tied neatly with laces in proportion on both sides and no dirt on them. He unclenched his fist: "You always wait for things to happen to you. You never, ever take charge of things. You never fix things on time, you never have money when I need it, you let dad back into the house to visit even though you said he couldn't. Why do you do these things? I hate having a loser family."

"Carlito," she began. "You have always strived for perfection. You look for order all around you. I didn't intentionally teach this to you. On your own you line up your shoes, you put your books heavier ones on the bottom, lighter ones on the top, you sharpen pencils every day. Sometimes, when people live with addicts they try to control their inner lives by keeping the external under control. It could be a way of compensating for what you feel you can't change. You are right. I let your father stay too long. I was afraid for him; sad for him, sad for us. I loved him once and having him move also meant giving up on a dream. It's very hard to admit failure especially in a marriage. It's hard to cut off a needy person and to start living independently.

"I have made mistakes Carlito, I am not perfect. I will make more mistakes. I ask your understanding in advance. This is life you know. It's a ride, an episode, a bunch of feelings and experiences that don't always coordinate well together. You haven't told me but maybe you have a girl right now that you like and she will bring things into your life. Some you will enjoy and embrace and other things you may want to change. But all the while you will be learning how to love and it will become more and more complicated, even if it isn't good and it gets deeper. Don't be so hard on me Carlito, I have tried very hard to be a good mother to you."

Carlito was in love. He had a 15-year old girl who wore her 10 year old sister's clothes, drank Slim Fast for breakfast, pickles for lunch and yellow cheese for dinner. Some days she fasted with water and tea. Carlito disliked fat women, uneducated women and mostly women without goals.

In the middle, or the beginning, or the mundane, the inconsequential, the unimportant, the window opened again. In a strip, horizontal wide and only a few inches long, a gateway in a line, the planets appeared and gray was the background as the planets rotated and swirled in a vortex. Not in the poetry; not in the lovemaking, but then it was by itself. Connected to the *allness* from a normal place of a wandering mind the universe gave Dina a gift ... the truth and it as not God by itself, but nature and God in it; God of it. It was all one and Cocaine, Will and Carlito were part of it and it was truth that there was a continuum of energy. And electricity between people couldn't be bound by paperwork and jewelry, but by their hearts and the feelings between them that were describable in small words that defined such a huge knowledge. How one wears her clothes, how pretty a face, or not, was not in real existence.

It wasn't real to consider money or furniture or polishing one's body. All that was there was the oneness of love and it was a given among the planets and in the window of the grayness there was light in the knowledge. Leopard print, pottery, tiles, mosaic designs now led to meditative places of peace in energy and like one huge orgasm death must be the most beautiful experience where she could let go; where she could live the real life of the other consciousness.

Dina felt small for abandoning Cocaine because of his mean addiction. Where was the physical to the spiritual transition on earth and how could she have done such a terrible thing to such a great man who was so sick.

She knew she was nothing in the something of the isness. Then as her desire to sex with a man was overridden by the insight of the universe she was tormented in thoughts of what was more important: Her soul? Her sex? or the collective consciousness? Was the allness focused on her as she was a representation of all of each one of every particle of life? Should she abandon herself the way Will had? The way her father had? Did Will know the world was not just about the bench in his backyard and the twigs he had to remove from the sidewalk around his house? That having two women who loved him was a gift? As love and beauty was in the universal agenda of how to live life; Einstein she had recalled said that the universe loved beauty and simplicity. But then both would need to be defined which brought her back to the subjective experience in her life of her family and her sex. And it was clear to her in fact it was now what she knew to be true that the laws of nature would always be the laws of man.

Henry the bartender called. Did she want to dance tonight – in the park – under the stars? She felt the breeze around her skirt; Vietnam war-baby princess yearning for her early lovers. This included the passed over Donald who taught to hold herself inside herself, inside himself. Maybe if he told about their sex he would still be alive. Hold it in, he held it in—all in – and after that couldn't tell secrets and let himself get killed rather than tell his father his secret. That he was not a soldier and he wasn't a student and he just wanted to fix cars at the family gas station.

Mother's funeral was over but Dina dreamt of her most nights: Eating pizza out of a large white box in the ocean with no land to be seen. Dina riding on Will's chest facing their faces together tasting his shoulder and it was delicious in its creaminess. Her nails digging into his back she always did this to him when they made love. In life he would pull her hand away but then in the dream he let her dig into him and his neck when he was inside of her. But in the dream he let her dig into his skin and his neck like he was butter. Tasting sweeter than when she was awake and he loved her in the dream as they could not separate from each other. Dina was envious of the dead around her in the real life as she saw the afterlife as the true life.

In the fine points in the gardens she saw the sculptures breathing. Each one alive, moving cylindrical round and round in their own space. Her room was a garden when she woke up . Filled with green vines, sweeping overhead many tiny leaves each one fat with life; earth life. And when the green plants turned brown and rotted into the earth it was understood that they would be reborn and so she knew it was the same with human souls too. Her mother who understood her passion so well that she looked the other way when she found her daughter's underwear behind the furniture, sent Dina messages and notes to help her to get the answers that she was looking for.

In a line, in a frequency, Will sent his undying love. He longed to put this head on her belly just to have his head rise and fall as she took in breaths of air. "Can you come here?" he asked, "I miss you. Can you please come?" And the words flew out his mouth and they were in long tones from his heart.

Dina's dreams leapt out of her. She was already there. The dream of flying over the tower on the beach in San Francisco was no dream. She would now fly to her Will and she would find the tower and look at the perfect sky and breathe the air that filled her cells with joy.

She will travel 3,000 miles to make love with him. He will touch her once, look into her eyes and she will rise and swell. She intends to love him. To watch how good he feels when he sees her. To see the smile designate across his face. Her spirit is ruby red. The 60's girl with the *lost woman life syndrome* was running off to her hippie. He was now a beautiful older man how could she ever tell him no. His soul was on hers when they were asleep. They met in the clouds and in the ocean and spit on each other's doubts. They are old souls reuniting in earth love. He needed her and confessed it. But so did Henry. But Will was in her element. The iron and sinews of her form, he was in there, but not Henry. Henry was the red of the wine, the sweet napkin he used to wipe her dripping face with.

Dina and Henry are dancing with sweat. He wants to be Henry Miller. He wants to write about his wandering cock; to be a man's writer. He watches Dina move. Her ass is wide and childbearing ready. He has never touched her there, in between not even over her clothes. Henry wants it. She knows. He is sure that she is sexy. She can be touched

anywhere and with his bartending
fingers he wants to slide his tips across
her. He dreams of her softened body
while Dina dreams of Will and waits for
him to return to say the words. Henry
makes her laugh in the swirl of a turning
cha-cha. Her hair flies in the sweaty
wind in the New York City hot night. He
wants his face in her breasts, his hands
around her back working it up then
down with deep kisses. She shakes her
skirt with the white eyelet rim at him but
she doesn't want him in her.

Henry gives Dina his work to
read. She wants the hands of the
fisherman, the gardener, his rough
callused hands on her baby city-white
skin, not the hands of the wine glass
cleaning, scotch serving bartenders.

She sweats like a flattened pearl.
Her white skin clashes against the night.
The darkness is a contrast for her laugh.
Her skin is wet, her hair in long black
strands cling to her pearled shoulders.
Henry wants to love her in bed and wrap
her in the sheet when they are done.
Henry is lovable but he has no appeal
for Dina. He is beautiful where Henry
Miller was not. He writes romantically

while Miller was unflowery and direct. He cannot be someone else even as he tries so hard not to be the bartender Henry from Bali's on West 53rd Street.

Dina takes only feelings; love feelings for her Will, who she will take as an old, tired, and unavailable body. For her he is the answer and in unregistered moments her Will memory comes and she can barely stand living when she thinks that it has been weeks since she has last seen him. That it can take more time more delays until she can hold him rushes into her boots. Blackness covers the soles of her feet. When? How long? Why?

Carlito skids into his dorm. The window over his desk shows him trees with curved branches, spider type legs attached to the trunks. The cocaine father stays in him, in his young veins pouring through his young, temperamental heart. He considers telling his father's ghost that he is sorry for his cruel words. But they would only be symbols with no meaning and the wrong intent. To purge himself from guilt but not to be sorry for the pain he caused his father. Carlito is ashamed of his father's memory. He is overwhelmed with embarrassment of his father's ashes in the Bronx sewer. He feels his father's laughter, hears the lemon sucking sounds from the curb.

Open the earth listen, listen, listen, listen to it move

an open. ing. Cry. ing. Earth. ling. <u>Dina Byrne Lopez</u>

Henry is chewing on her skirt. Her knees are licked. The slip is wet and he is a young dog on his mother's milk. He chews upward then his nose is on her cap. The knee slightly bony, slightly tanned from summer washing side walking. He can feel the warmth from in between her legs. "This isn't good for us," she says. She knows that she is rarely a casual lover. Dina loves with her home. Fourth house, fixed sign, eighth house dominated chart a lover of rebirth and death. She can be a whore to her lover but she is no whore. No bitch. But a bitch in passion in orgasm she is the bitch but not out of routine; not out of the street. She remembers Cocaine. How the world descended on his coke fluted body when he died on the sidewalk. Henry loved Dina without alcohol without an old memory. He expected only the experience from her. With her new skirt and her apple, soft, and delightful and he knew this before his fingers went inside her; before his chew gently nipped inside her thigh.

She pushes his face away from her now as he inches toward her where the in between voice speaks to her racing heart. She doesn't love Henry. Now on the couch her c-cup overflows. The secret is out. No need to pretend. She is starving to be loved. Prod her. But he, her Will, is nowhere. Not here. He cannot take her onto his chest. So she becomes her own lover. Her sex is. Her love for her is. The other…an instrument? The mouth: the tongue. She knows by the kiss. And Henry has no kiss. For her; he cannot kiss her and turn her on and she knows this is not love but sex. And sex is good. She hits it because it is her body. Not Cocaine's. Not Will's or Henry's but Dina's body is hers and she can have orgasm and fly and peak out because she can do that and she knows herself and knows what to look for and when it hits, when she finds it she goes to the blind space in the world of joy, pure bliss, ecstasy beyond wonderful food or beauty and that is seen with her eyes. Framed art, unframed music will never give her this perfect field of pure happiness.

She feels Cocaine's anger. No one else should get to smell her. Will's tongue brings emotional and soul orgasm as she declines her anti-climax memories of the best come waving across her in baby tsunamis.

Henry sits on the bed. His back is broad. He is tall. Hair curls around his ears, a big blond boy with city car exhaust behind his ears. Big and quiet and in his eyes is the lover who she knew centuries ago-that thought flashes across her tired brain. He reaches again for her and her nipples are chilled and circular little nurturers. She looks down as he gets on. Then he grabs her whole breast and swallows her in his mouth. She is flushed. Henry has the prize; he is falling in love, falling into possession. Flying into heaven as it is on earth.

Will doesn't speak to her on the phone and the dreams tell him to and he feels the love of her and he wants it for himself. The whole cake; he wants to eat it all, not to share a piece with anyone else. He is silent with his truth. Wanting. Needing to be open. Wanting. Needing to be seen as open. Then, he is seen and understood as a closed-off man as unavailable and contrary: Carefree and uncaring so Dina trusts her magic and her knowing.

When she says to him: "I love you, I love you, I love you," he cups his hands over his ears. When she isn't looking and he jumps off the bed; avoiding the blessing of being loved, as he lives in the torture the delicious pain of wanting to conquer the unlovable wife. He lives in locked freedom. He holds onto his wife's elbow. It digs into his hands the same ones that make Dina sweat. He wants to smell of Dina so in front of the wife he can dream of his lover. The scent is washed off for now. Her hair no longer rides under his nose. When she comes and walks toward him he will hold her and he will smile into her face and he will know that he does love her.

Dina visits Will. She makes it to California where they scatter around San Francisco. He takes her two towns north so he can kiss her in public. He follows her into the women's room into the stall. He wants to fuck her in there and he does; very quickly. Her ass is fleshy and white. She grabs onto the door and he is in from behind. They know. They can. Do this: Forever. She flushes the rubber down the toilet and it swirls down and around the restaurant public bathroom. They are starving and eat chicken and potatoes from each other's plates. Cold water washes the bitterness after they suck the bones. Will can hardly get enough of her. When he has finished her clitoris stays on his fingers. He still hears her yelling. Her mouth and girlish teeth that hold the same girlish expression from twenty years ago charges him. Will takes her on the side and he rolls her over onto her waist sinking his hands into her abdomen that is full. He grabs it, Cups it; holds it like she is to eat; the guided Long Island fisherman who sees the world poetically. She reads her words to him. He tightens her up when he grabs her stomach. Her center rises with trust and joy and the whispers begin: "I've missed you. We can't be apart like this anymore. Can we do this? Can you move to California? In Will's words her poetry expands. He unsnaps her bra, licks her nipple then there is no world.

She thinks all day long. For hours she watches smoke rise from the incense in the dusty mirror over the table. Straight up. There is no wind so the smoke goes straight to darken the ceiling. Her lover, her Will, hides in the volume of the music. Her heart bangs in its rightful box. Their legs blend. Sticks. Friction. Sweet lime. Her shoulders crystallize under his mouth there is no holding onto her flow. Her intelligence. Her epoxy led him to the vast veins of her mind with the spirals that spark with color. He cannot separate her body from her mind.

A shadow across her back reminds him of the hills in August: Beige, round and in perfect lines where the shadow starts curving across her skin. She is the carrier the symptom less bearer of his land. She's front down. Nose partially buried and Will warming her nudeness. Her gender is her nationality. Her inheritance is her womb.

Dina is American and she is Latin American and she is Polish and she is African and Parisian and Asian. Dina is a hormonal species of human in the female gender, a planetary woman a giver of milk and time and money: A bed maker and a brewer of fine tea. She has hemmed the clothes and scrubbed the stains. She is from Haiti and Spain. Dina is a woman from Barbados. She holds her hips wide for sitting cross legged on the floor; she keeps her mouth painted red. Ear rings. Let them dangle from her lobes. Plant her in Siberia or Europe she will warm the bread. Walk her in Ethiopia and her breasts will keep her children from famine. She is the shield in Ireland from the English Protestants blasts. She is only a girl; nothing else. She is her womb. It plasters in her hair the way she thinks and the deep fuck that rises out of her. That fuck is not Irish or African, but woman.

The war killed her mother. It took thirty years for the bombs and the cutting sounds of khaki helmets as bullets put the white part of baby's brains across the land. Fertilizing the rice patties, nurturing rattan stalks in exchange for medals of Honor in velvet boxes that snapped onto the American mother's fingernails.

Mother sold nurses and waitress uniforms in Valley Stream, the center of Long Island in a store that was owned by a Jewish family. She'd straighten out darts across the chests of store mannequins. Every day she was lucky and she would say that she was because her son was a "D" classification from a leg injury that caused him to limp. She was guilty. And her mouth the shape of it turned down, down, downward further and further and then she looked like a sad clown. Every day the killed boys were her sons and she couldn't separate herself from the other mothers, and each dead boy was hers as they lied in the mosquito dampness with their body parts still jumping 200 feet away not knowing that they were supposed to be dead.

Dina was on the verge of getting it. The place that she kept missing that she knew was there. The space she found when meditation gave the answer. When it felt like the answer to all. Where she didn't follow anyone and the words were not there to tell her what it was.

The place where she stopped asking questions and life was with space and isness. Her angst quieted, her voices listening and waiting for the great answer to the quiet, the bridge to life in a drop of water and she understood that there was room for all of life, the solar system, the universe and hers and Will's hearts in that droplet.

She wanted Henry to be in there with her, in a separate life away from the bar, and the family, and the demands on the body. Henry had been tending bar for months and he knew Dina deeper than she could see. "So you think?" she began, "if we looked really hard we could see their souls?"

Henry put a glass that he had cleaned on the drain board, both arms on the bar then he leaned into her and said, "Yes, I believe we could." Both of his eyes looked into her. She looked right back. Whether it was thought of spirit Donald was there with her. Sweet and memorable she loved the secret he kept. Saint Donald whose parents moved away from the house they raised him in after he was blown up by a napon bomb in Vietnam.

His fingertips are dancing with ice. Tappety, tap, tap across her waist. She lies in bed on her side when the icy touches drop onto her. He cannot get warm. His lips are chilling on the back of her neck. He works his face around to her front his fingers working her waist. She stretches her body arches her legs and opens them so he can touch her there. Her sweet mound the hairs are wet in a soppy like jelly. A thick liquid sloshes and sloshes and sloshes making that noise, giving that scent that she gets when she is sexing. It's undeniably hers that he smells and she can't but he can and he does and he now is ready as he has been for a long time. He kisses her lips. He kisses her in between her legs. She is firm and her clitoris stands up and he is on her and she cannot think of anything until the lovemaking has faded. So she hits the place from the physical dimension and the world is gone and is on pause while Dina does what she can do.

Let Dina be a whore. Better a breathing whore than a dead virgin. But the brother who cannot fight is a crown prince in the Byrne home. He is kissed and told everyday how lucky they are to have him. How sad it is that the other sons have been taken from their mothers and killed for no reason. The brother, stuck to his mother's cherry cries miserably at her funeral and the umbilicus goes to the grave with her. It rings out from her corpse for years and he freezes on Dina's couch like Cocaine Baby accustomed to ice particles leaking from his nose.

His head was an open book from one side the one view the back.

It opened and it said I love you and I knew it was true.

The front was full faced and you stood there smiling. <u>Dina Byrne Lopez</u>

The Bangladeshi doctor at the day job, Dina's outside of poetry income source, examines her lungs. Corporate day job that pays her rent and fills Carlito's cereal bowl and keeps the milk sweet. She is tired and worn and wants to sleep her days into the nights into the days into the nights into the winter and into the spring and sleep through the summer and wait for the fall season when the days start to shorten with daylight. With his stethoscope he listens to her heart. His hand went on her shoulder and her back and she could only remember Will by the Bengali's touch. That Will's heart was slow and that was a disappointment to her. His call to ask her, "Are you okay?" and then his words and the image and where his hand was when he asked her…"are you sleeping with anyone else?"

"You can't ask me that. You are still married and you are not here." Then she thought about the purity of the doctor and his cold fingers on her back and how he pressed into her collar bone staying there longer than he needed to until she shrugged a bit to shake him off. He asked her if she was married. "I have a cough," she answered, "Can you give me something?" The Bengali knew she was not married because Cocaine's death was well known. His eyes in her memory were brown, looking a bit smaller than they were from his glasses.

Will needs her womanness. He wanted to hold her in the bed and stick his fingers in. He never asked. He never wanted to warm up first. He coiled like a cobra around her neck and her back until his hands without thought were in where she was alive.

In dripping honey a conversation began. Henry came over to Dina's place. They ate spaghetti that kept falling off Dina's fork onto the front of her. She could now smell of tomato and basil, sweet and salty across the pale yellow shirt she wore. It had streams of orangey red like happy worms that had danced across her. Henry wanted to philosophize about mentally ill people. He wanted answers. "Are they wired differently? Do they fall in love?" And most of all…"Do they like who they are?"

She didn't need to think to have answers. Just feel it and this time she dangled her earrings with her fingers and held onto her hair in one big loop. She was in her Will mind of missing him. And this occasional lover in front of her, eating without dropping food onto him was a good way to spend time. To forget how she was really feeling. Will disabled her heart. He kept her in his

pink ocean. Where were his hands now
that she needed them?

> *I am in a poet's dream logged in*
> *between science and art.*
>
> *Leaving on a jet plane slamming*
> *into heaven's seat*
>
> *Disabling my heart once again.*
> <u>*Dina Byrne Lopez*</u>

She wanted Henry to get what he
wanted from her. Answers, contrary or
agreeable, either way he wanted mental
stimuli. She needed him to love her after
the food was gone. On the couch where
Cocaine's feet stretched out in front of
him or in the bed that she moved a few
times since Cocaine had died. They
stopped talking after the last half
swallows of red wine.

Dina lies on the couch. Alone.
Her pulse jumps with her thoughts. Her
life is ruled from her childhood space.
Dying, everyday during her undeveloped
life – the early life – the girl time
sabotaged by her father who loved her

more than she was to know, as much as a father could.

Her father left her alone with her pain: To know her own feelings as he could not coddle her in his life. Only in the dreams could he find her and love her with a father's soul. And he thought she always knew as he knew that she was his favorite person. The wanted child; a planned child and that should have been the answer he believed. He knew how much he loved her and so then the whole world should. He took her to fine restaurants and taught her how to order and he taught her about good clothes and gave her classical music and books from Havelock Ellis, to Abe Hirschfield, Doystofesky and Eugene Burdick and Henry Miller and Mary McCarthy and always the library and the Book of the Month Club and when she hated him she would write to him in his books that she felt that way and he would never get back to her. He ignored her writing to him on the borders of the pages in his books. The words were embedded there forever in his favorite books and feelings toward him so he took the beatings from his much loved child. Harry James, Peer Gynt,

Sarah Vaughn, he filled the house of hatred with the volume of his favorite artists when he was home until Dina disappeared into her room with the flowered wall paper. Pink posies and fine green stems were abundant and she could smell them from their flat dimension. By the third grade she could distinguish through the love of her father the masters that he insisted she know as his greatest fear for his great creation was that she should turn out to be common; to be typical, or to be ordinary.

The on the couch, in the dark, the early father in his white tee shirt spoke out under his arm as the smell of his sweat from working she could smell.

Cocaine loved her. The progressive baby that she was would kindly suck him off in his sleep. Poetry that she wrote to her father migrating in her thoughts as she pursed her lips together. Cocaine loved to wake up that way, coming by his lover; by his wife. She would fill her mouth up with his sweet dick, lubrication lining her mouth then his release and he so happy in the sexual spiritual moments – married lovers – in the good old days before cocaine like her father's scotch took him away from her. When his dick stayed soft until the cocaine wore off she would fall asleep until he was on top of her fucking her in her grogginess. Waking up to him coming in her she felt like she had missed the whole thing. Out of breath he would drool on her chest while her nipples remained the same. Her breasts then longed for love. Cocaine Baby would pass off away to the sky and the great Indian clouds of memory and forgiveness. Wonderful buffalo images with Aztec prints honored his Puerto Rican Indian blood. Intoxication, a woman's rejection could not tap that memory away. The one from his mother, the Reyes family from Mayaguez, Puerto Rico the politicians of the island who coveted intelligence and addictions, for the brothers it was okay. They could drink and talk and fuck all night long. And Cocaine was proud until gravity showed him and all the family who was the real boss when he fell off the roof in New York City.

Dina dreams of seeing him on a wild horse's back riding into heaven across the clouds. The answers are in the elements she believes. In our breath the real answers are never found. She speculates and she examines and she considers and she dreams. She knows she is limited and that time has no favorites.

Her father's earth face disappeared one afternoon in January behind the gray brick house in the center of Long Island. His life and his music that went in one way and out one of the three other ways closed that day and he would never again gain entrance to his house. Her mother and father made love, made sex, made children in the 1950's, before Vietnam was known as a place to send young American children to get killed. They made instant coffee together over a plastic tablecloth on the kitchen table. They watched each other's bodies wilt and cream into their reclining chairs next to racks of Look Magazine, the Ladies Home Journal and Playboy. Everyone thought that father would die first. He drank too much alcohol and he was mean spirited toward his wife in his stupor. He was sexy to her when he was drunk. He was aggressive in bed, forceful and his face was on her all over her soft, post-

Victorian body. And for all the cruelty he gave her, he knew how to take care of her body better than she did. And they both enjoyed his power in bed. A bull dozer: Banging, hammering, he could hold off until her soft, sweet sober body jumped with rivers of joy. Multi levels she swore it was finding love of her man, unlike Dina who *came* and found bliss and purity of consciousness. Mother thought she could only orgasm with her husband and the idea of him having that power turned her on more and more.

Northeast America sends her roots toward the sky to recover from her lost family. The democratic government pretends to be lonely for socialized approaches to life.

On the job, her job, Will calls. There is time he says to love. Her heart races and she loses sight of the day job. "I have been tending to her and we are okay for now. Not entirely unhappy. I have hope that she can recover. I have to believe that she will make it. There's a job I'm thinking of taking in Wisconsin. The move would be very good for both of us." He said that his wife could continue her therapy there and he could make a good income and have other benefits as a local union organizer.

All that, Dina thinks, and no pussy. The dry loveless marriage was suddenly anointed in pretend marital bliss. The happy couple would move to the center of the United States ... Will and the Peruvian. Her gauze wrapped legs, the clicking of the wife's cane on the cemented sidewalks as she holds one arm bent inward, her flattened head of hair from sleeping on one side too long, the drooling mouth and the crabby personality.

Dina wants to send him to hell. She thinks in emotional clichés. She hushes her spirit, killing it, putting her love to its death. She is terrified to tell him how she feels so she lies. Lies. Lies. Lies.

Seeds in the air with wanton wings she keeps her mind with her mother today. The mother of all mothers visits Dina's garden.

Chapter 6

The weekend arises out of time. She hears a din from the Atlantic Ocean. She rides on top of the sun in the city afternoon swearing her love for Will. He is the only magic in her life. Now that her life is self dependent the answers and obedience to Cocaine are in thought form. Henry will know, and she will remind him that no one can be like Will in her. Henry finds his way back into Dina's moments.

There is no time to watch her father. He calls her, "Can you come here. When can you come here?" he wants to know. He would rather see her and wants her to take care of him instead of his son; the son whose mother pinned Band-aids inside his pockets so he would be prepared if he got hurt. There is no wind around the father's life only fire and only matches and friction from beer and *Chivas*, and hot seats from Hansen's bar on Passion Street from forty years ago. The seats stay hot in his mind and on the steering wheel of his car.

Dina is loyal to Dina, especially now that she has the doctor, Arun, who listens to her and holds her hands and takes off her shirt and knows and understands the tips of her breasts. He can't help himself he says. He apologizes over and over that he is so attracted to her as a woman. He says he cannot treat her as a patient any longer. His soft hair is cut so the front of it hits the beginning of his brow. Dina wipes a few of the strands out of his eyes. He is twelve years younger than she is. He is now her lover. She cannot see Will before her. He has receded into the cave of sleeping and lost hands. Will appears when she holds Henry. When she is finished making love with Henry Will becomes the focus. His face. His voice. His touch. His fuck. But now with the doctor it is the loving and it is not connected to any memory of another it is without static. Now all the love experience pours out of her bottle. He is only a man. That is all he ever wanted to be. He isn't thinking right now. He takes her bra straps and slides them under his fingers. He takes off her clothes and he looks at her nipples and European womanly breasts.

"My father is dying," she tells Arun. He takes his fingers off her and holds her in his arms. His office is dim from dark furniture, heavy curtains, and overstuffed leather arm chairs.

"I have two daughters," he says. "I, like your father, love them more than the air. They are princesses. Perfect. Father's love their daughters that way."

"I see him walking when he is dead. I have day dreams of him dead and walking around and around in a hospital gown and his knees skinny and the hair worn off, gone from pants rubbing against his skin for seventy-five years. He struggles to live. He struggles to die," she says.

The father's house is quiet and cushioned in rugs and large fat wooden tables. The doors to the rooms are hard to close; the windows are decorated with crusted spiders and brittle leaves that have blown inside from the oak trees. They are frozen against the screens. His non-academic child shows up to cook and clean for him. He lives in the house of death. He has doors without knobs and a cumulus heart that beats and collides when he says, "Don't leave me alone."

He doesn't listen to the movements on her face. He can't hear her head turn away from his needs. He doesn't listen, cannot hear her crying or see her wet face when she whispers behind her cheek, "You're already dead." The difficult daughter, the poet, the disappointment to him who could only sing and dance and write while he drove his Buick, Riviera and entombed himself in carcinogens from his Kent cigarettes.

The walls of the father's house smell of him. When you walk into his house you know that the walls have known him for a long time. They know his thoughts and they know the way his blood smells. The rags in his house know who he is. There is not a dish nor a fork nor a space on his wall-to-wall carpet that doesn't watch him. The mirrors are only to be found in the bathrooms and the bedrooms and they are there out of choice as no other reflection he believes should know where he is.

His windows are his encapsulation. They breathe in, like he, rotted air expelling from his internal war. They catch his tears in their voices and in the sounds that have lived there for fifty years. In the tiny cracks that felt the mother's last breath, as her exhale seeped through and countered Dina's world and Dina's direction, when the unfolding came Dina caught her mother's breathe. Into her it swallowed her and with Carlito it was passed through again. Then he accepted his new life now that his nana was gone.

The father is giving birth to his ghost. He is with an unwanted pregnancy. He waits for the pain and is looking for a portal, an easy one where he can slide through the door as he did in life on windy days. But the wind is not for him. He is to blend with the fire and to be buried in the sand. His legs will bounce through the rooms and down the steps. An eternity in the sound and it will stay in the cement and in the wood and it will be remembered by the crow that watches from the oak. The belly of the bird is cold when the father skips into the other world. The brother's feet fall aside and become unfrozen. He will join the crow and they will feel each other's hearts as the father leaves the house. The father, who didn't want to be alone to love the walls in each of his rooms. Each color salutes him and respects his desires. He wanted a meal, a dance, a newspaper, a toilet, a chair, a refrigerator door left open on a hot day to discuss the coils as a possibility of its breakage.

Then he thought about his only son, the male child from his union with his wife who labored almost two days to give life to him. And as the father's ghost labored into the world and the pain in his lungs grew and became big, he had visions of sex. In the rebirth he wondered if he would get another taste. It didn't have to be ice cream in July, or the tenderness from the old woman who taught him how to play the violin just before he turned thirteen. And now he was worried that he would be thinking about those things and not his children before he died and how could that be? Their inheritance abandoned by his emotional distractions. His humor misunderstood as cruel sarcasm and the cursed premise of his life. He was, and he would be remembered as a bastard; a mean frown-faced man whose love felt like a splinter under a dead man's heel.

Dina is lonely. Her father taught her this emotion. He nurtured it in her with his blindness; with his hush. The house where her father learned about the sun she was swallowed in loneliness. She lonelied in there; she cried in there. In the house where her Valentine's Day voice bounced off the attic roof she could feel her old loneliness: The lonely that taught her how to play hide-and-seek in between Cocaine Baby and Carlito. She didn't feel ready for the lonely to come in. It wasn't time for it to surface: The lonely for Will; the lonely for her mother; the lonely for her son, the lonely for her poetry in the gray spaces of her life. The lonely where Will put his hands on her head, on her back where he covered her in his breath causing her to sigh great big sighs that rose out of the lonely for Will place memory.

The father gives his tenderness by leaving Dina most of his things: The books, the ones where she wrote that he was a bastard, when she was ten-years-old. The bastard kept them. He knew. In him he knew, in him he understood, the bastard knew that she was a poet. The bastard loved the poet daughter. He saw her bold, assertive nature like his. He wanted two children like him. Two who were more talented and forceful and different even though he was a business man. A man who lived his life doing business, he felt differently on the inside. He wanted to write, but instead he read; he wanted to dance, but instead he watched. He wanted to sing, but instead he listened; he wanted to act, but instead he dreamt; he wanted to garden, but instead he shopped. He wanted to be a lover, but instead he kept quiet; stayed still, afraid to be a fool and never to be seen or to see himself. Instead he died a lonely in the lonely and Dina lived his talent. His shit swarming around on the grout, lips suckered on the tile floor. He hated it, shamed it. Then he was in the shower when he fell and his body absorbed body dirt from the floor and his body covered the drain and the water built up and flooded over the lip of the shower and onto the bathroom floor and seeped through the house.

He was finally released. His chest stopped rising and lay flat like the plain land around his house. The few hairs on his face stopped pushing out toward the lightened sky. He released himself from himself. The nights were no longer nights in the night sky. Night was now in the daytime and the mid-time and alone time and busy time. Blue night sky closed the father's eyes shut with permanent glue over his lids. The beast scampered out of his mouth and laughed at his journey.

There are memories of cheeseburgers on large seeded rolls from the local bakery. No name brand bottles of soda layered in crates waiting for next summer's fourth of July. The brother opens his knees and now he can come up for air. The father sleeps but his children wait for him to wake up. He isn't really dead. He is not truly gone: His heart pounds in the house where the crow flew to a lower branch; a bird's eye view that has seen and has watched the aftermath of a war from forty years ago. The dead mother borrows the crow's eyes so she can watch her family change. She wants the son to take off his bandages. The brother arrives at the

house where the gate doesn't close
from icy molecules that stand by like
soldiers of time. He catches the sun that
causes the icy water to drip and he
looks for his father's prints, foot prints,
hand prints, mind prints, soul prints.
Dead prints compromise his dreams of
acceptance in the desert of death.

He steals the fury of his father in
gold brilliance. Spiraling into grace he
seeks to forgive and to understand the
father's rage. The disappointment of a
life lived on the fringe of loving yet never
to let the world know that he had found it
to keep the evidence of love to himself
for his fear was to be seen as weak like
a plant infested with mites. Weak like
Virginia Wolf who put rocks into her coat
pockets and walked into the water that
was above her head. Weak like the
longing in his heart that was so deep
and wet if he allowed himself to feel love
in a loving and love full way, he would
die. In the beginnings of love resolved in
his fantasy of letting love release to
bloom into the world he faded and faded
until it was understood in the physical
world that he was finally gone.

There is water in the basement flowing, overflowing into the walls by the windows. It is time; time to go forward. There is no dignity in drowning in the father's house. He is already dead. He has not said good bye the way Dina wanted him to. She wants to tell him about her husband that he was a cocaine baby; a dependent addict, a longer, a lover, a monger, a hoarder of cocaine and that her husband loved cocaine more than he loved her, or Carlito, or himself.

Cocaine Baby loved cocaine the way the father loved scotch. The liquid fire that burnt a hole in his filter and compromised his life so much that he learned to live in the ache his whole life of holding back his tears.

Dina wants to tell her father that she married *him*. She was doubly angry as the water filled the basement and that he was dead and wouldn't get to see it. Just like him to avoid problems; to leave. To be too drunk with death to notice and to know that she was left to deal with a flood.

She wanted him to see her that she was whole and that as a whole woman she could handle him and the grieving. Her father wanted to think about her, but he only saw her one way, not the whole way. He discovered her but couldn't uncover her because of his failings; because of her artistic nature. She drifted into lights and into oceans and onto rocks. She loved in a stupor of loving for days and lived her life in the consciousness of love.

Her poetry is out in a book. A collection of poetry bound tightly with a garden of flowers on the cover. It comes to life as her father struggles with his bruises. Her love, her abandonment, her grief is in there. Her Carlito is the ribbon. He holds her together. He sinews through the family as the grand finale. They now consider Carlito, the baby, the inheritor of Dina's feelings of the Vietnam incident. That he was never taught how to fight was never allowed a toy gun because of his mother, because of that war.

Over the cobblestones peeking each button opened.

Then my tongue gets stuck on the subway pole. Dina Byrne Lopez

Throwing herself into the lonely, Dina washes herself in the astounding aloneness that is the lonely. Will pulls it out of her when he sees her.

"Are you okay?" he says. Her loneliness is a badge of a new life. She scrubs with it in the bathroom in lonely soap. Dina's strands of hair are weeping memories of love. Washing, and soaping away the dead love into the new loneliness. Capturing the lost, watching it swirl into the drain of the bathtub. There was no holding on, only letting go: Only welcoming the birth of loneliness; the resurgence of the self. She was in her loneliness only a woman, a cog that closed her eyes from a vertigo simulation.

She was alive only to her. Not to the walls. Not to the water, or to Carlito, or to Will. Only she knew where she was. Dina in the aloneness of her lonely she would breathe and palpitate in the water in the lotion that she put on her face. Brushing her hair was lonely. Curling her lashes was a lonely in the aloneness of the mirror while she alone looked back into the lonely self of Dina.

The skirt snapped onto her waist above her hips rounding out her thighs. Dina's sex was a filtered voice in her love memory where her lonely sex appeared out of storage. Will knew in the darkened room where she was with it. "I am terribly lonely for you," she says. "I can't stop the loneliness for you even when I am with others. It stays and it stays. It only stops when you hold me." Food dried in her mouth; gone, emotionless, unfeeling spinach. No volume in the dinner the steak less, steak. No aroma, no life, only dead food that falls into her mouth and out of her heart lining her chew, smiling all the way down into her swallow but missing the purpose. No feeling only death in the aloneness of the lonely and without him there was no taste.

She gets whiter in the darkened room. The black shirt makes her alabaster; the one that slips over her head then falls across her rounded front with a square neckline. In her white skin Will is reminded of untouched Irish virgins: The types who tuck their catechisms under their armpits and tickle each other on Sunday afternoons, after church: Loose haired girls who giggle at curse words and place their hands over their exposed crooked teeth.

Dina shoved herself into him and he put his mouth on her shoulder. His white skinned flower that he could not do without. Her smell on his hands, he licked his fingers and pushed her down and put his face in between her legs. Her perfect flesh the pollen of her orgasm this night, wide and mountainous flesh he bites into and delights his tongue along her lips bathing the protector of it all.

They sleep on her wooden bed. Solid fat mattress filled with sleep before they settle in. The smell of city sidewalks of car exhaust, truck diesel greets Dina's morning dream. She was watching a rambling house with people running about with no roof. Beams crossed over in a triangle, but no roof. So she stares at the white ceiling and she hears Will's breath and feels his body work to keep it alive with oxygen.

Her shirt is loose and exposes her right breast. She wonders about Will; his heart, the heart in his body and the one in his head. Does he hear the clicking of the sick wife's cane when he sleeps? Does he feel his fingers around her? He rolls over toward her. His wide fisherman sunned and weathered face is unaware of the deep wrinkle down his forehead. Hairs curl out of his nose. He kisses her face.

"Carlito called," she says. "He's coming home. I told him yes come home. He's my baby love, you know, my precious Carlito. In the morning of a ceiling less rumination of her dream home, she sees herself making food for Carlito – meats, spaghetti, chocolate cake – she smiles to think of how he will eat. Fast to get full. He will trust his mother to make the best for him; sweet cake and tender meat. A nap will follow and his long legs will slide off his bed. He will cover his mother in tears; Cocaine Baby's son. Carlito was his heart. Everything for Carlito, but only after the cocaine: Cocaine, Carlito then Dina.

The house has photographs of Carlito as a baby. In different areas on tops of tables, by the dresser mirror, on a kitchen shelf, smiles of Carlito in colors and in black and white. The phone rings out of their morning ferment. "I will call you later," she says to Henry. She then remembers his quick movement, body smell, long blond hair and the way he loved her.

Her head is her womb. The face is pure womb organ. That internal hidden part of her body is exposed, known, made evident to the world. She was still looking for cocaine's poison. The addiction ached in her body and caused her to say words and to feel things and to demonstrate how she wasn't able to fully love in one swoop of communication.

A chime from the corner church on First Avenue rang eight times before she stopped counting. Will was taking off her shirt over her head. From the window the sky looked orange and the joy of the lightened room pacified her. Then she was bare before him. He learned how to take her clothes off her body with patience.

She would look into his eyes then she would put her lips on his face and say, "Now." Four of his fingers would go inside her finding her damp and familiar

and he was always comfortable in there.
She would push down onto his hand,
climb onto him and find his sweet taste
by his ears and his nipples darkened
against his skin.

Cocaine Baby was a picture
across her thoughts. She wouldn't look
when the police came. Only cry.
Scream. Wail out from the pain center.
Where could she go? Nowhere to go to
leave the pain on the couch or in her
living room where Cocaine Baby would
nod off; and in the same room where he
beat her. Her sex is wasted on time. Her
sex is wasted on nothing on waiting for
another. Her spirit is lined in her sex. A
cave of film under her skin over her
bones causing both to pull him onto her.
Good sex. Sex alone, sex in the forest
with no light. The beat from her heart is
strong and the heart stopped trembling.
The beat filled with loving pink with red
stars on it. Will was phasing into the
phase of love with her.

It was a good time for love
against the father's secrets. Then a
delicious Chinese dinner: Sesame
chicken, snappy green peas, rice, white

and Dina's skin a bit tanned as her fingers reached for a noodle. They kissed more after the food. He grabbed her ass on the street while they were walking in the night air, blackened city streets dramatized by City street lights, shadows moving with the sounds of their feet.

"If she hadn't gotten sick would you have left her for me?" This is what she asks Will during a walk home with all the confidence that an adult orphan can have.

"Not instead. I would not have left her for you, but if she passes I would consider you as a partner. I can't leave. Not now."

Not ever is what Dina heard; what she knew. Pull. Pull in. Pull close. The other. Fill it with flowers. Fill it with oranges. Take it aside. Make it last. The boat. It crashed. No resurrection could be tried. She fell down. Then, she was in the sand – the quick sand the ankle deep knee sucking deep water-soaked sand.

Then the life of a woman whose sex life was ordinary as it entwined with men in her physical journey. Her father now gone and no longer in front of her to be replaced by men who will love her as a woman only: Not as their child as he did. The leaders in the music of her soul were Cocaine Baby who tied his knot into her dress. She transitioned in her life with him from her father who drank his life away until the birds flapped their wings outside his house. He pulled down the shades to hide but they looked in anyway. When he surrendered and she knew he was gone she could admit her story as she looked down in between herself and at first would see Cocaine Baby. His face was branded across hers. His music covered the walls in her bedroom. She begged him to leave and when he did her father was on the other side. Will and Henry delved into her and waited for the husband on her face to disappear. Arun, the doctor her Bangladeshi lover has no other. His ex wife is still in Bangladesh and his children are there with her. He cannot stop touching Dina's white skin; he pulls it into a soft pucker in between his fingers. His eyes are excited. He gets sexy from her skin. The feel, the alabaster the woman underneath it: Her words turn him into her life. He begs her to let him in to let him into her and allow him to sit and stare at her. At the way her breasts form underneath her shirt. The way her hair curls down them her dark hair like a Bengali woman. Then her red lips over her white teeth; teeth that she cleans for his kiss. To bite his chin and to suck his ears with until his dick flies out of his pants. It is strong and it is wide and it is compared to Cocaine Baby's and to Will's and to Henry's and his eyes are in love with her and that look to her is good enough. The look she sees in his eyes when he looks at her. The look when he can't stop looking at her and falling in love with her. He pulls her onto him to sit on him. She lets him have his way and he makes her wet and she wants to let him have his way because he has that look of loving her and because he hasn't been fucked for so long and she knows that. His shoes sweat. He pushes the dick to spread Eastern cum, finding her American and sweet piece the most delicious he has ever had. He cums with his mind and his memory of his wife who didn't do it like this. Who pushed him away while his heart beat with anticipation and then he would sadly go to sleep without any. No sex from the sexless wife that he loved. His dick that was hard most nights had finally met its dream.

Arun wants the fuck to go somewhere. He wants to take her out. Can they go away for a weekend together and look at sail boats on the North Shore. They will throw bread to the geese. They can hold hands while taking slow steps by the bay. He wants to smell her clothes. He wants to smell her in the middle of the night when the toxins slowly pour out of her. Then he wants to smell her again when she has coffee in the morning and eats toast. He wants to see her smell. To run his pink tipped fingers along her neck and curl his mind around her breasts that fill up when he gets close to her.

That night after she and Arun were married, his eyes were filled with black passion. He could drive her on him and she would be happy. The pain came in her stomach and when she cried it was from there the place she learned to speak from. The eye in her belly cried, heaving great sounds of loss. Love of Will was not in her heart but in her center in the core of her body where she would digest the pain of loss from where she ate. Now her new husband, her special lover was on her, his breasts, his youth and his optimistic ideas and believing that Dina knew it was time to let go.

Now say good bye to the eyes that she looked into in absence. Time to remember to forget to let it go and that the moments that died off moved along, forward to be buried in the grave next to Cocaine Baby. The dream of loving Will was in the closet of secrets next to Vietnam and Donald. Time had run out, run along, and run amok.